STO

W9-DEY-620

FRIENDS
OF ACPL

3 1833 00704 7498

PAWPAW'S RUN

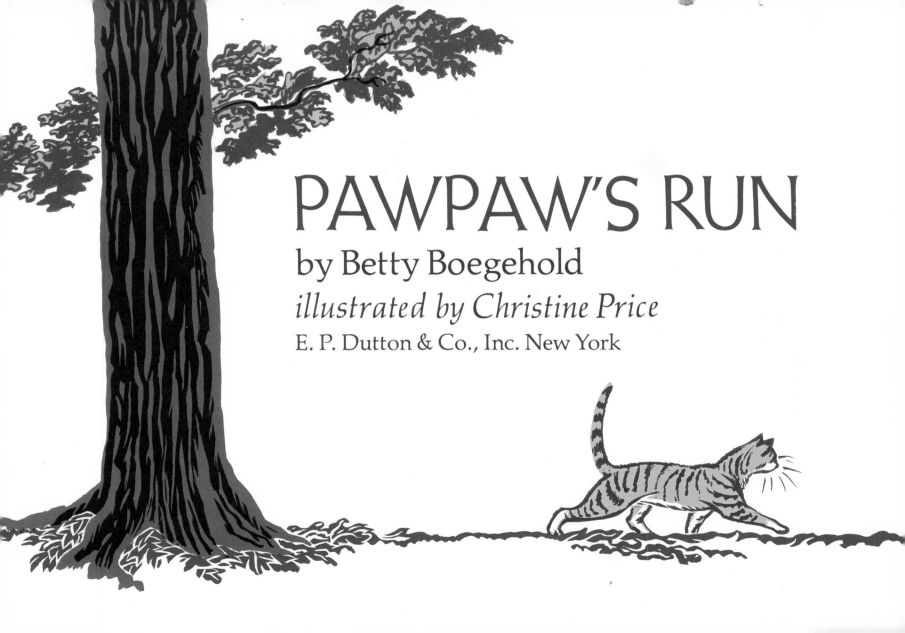

PAWPAW'S RUN

by Betty Boegehold

illustrated by Christine Price

E. P. Dutton & Co., Inc. New York

Text copyright © 1968 by Betty Boegehold
Illustrations copyright © 1968 by Christine Price
All rights reserved. Printed in the U.S.A.

No part of this book may be reproduced in any form
without permission in writing from the publisher, except
by a reviewer who wishes to quote brief passages in con-
nection with a review written for inclusion in a maga-
zine, newspaper, or broadcast. Published simultaneously
in Canada by Clarke, Irwin & Company Limited,
Toronto and Vancouver.

Library of Congress Catalog Card Number: 68-13417

First Edition

For Julie

SO. SCHOOLS
C698052

Pawpaw hunts in the forests,
Down where the rabbits run—
A moonlit cat in the meadow,
A golden cat in the sun.

The owl's round eyes blink slowly
As Pawpaw slips through the grass,
The meadow mice safe in their holes
Watch as the padded paws pass.

For a night and a day, and a night again
Pawpaw has hunted alone.
In the green Ohio wilderness,
Cat-free and wild he has run.

Now, from the woods by the river,
He comes to the wilderness road,
Over the tracks of the wagons
He comes again to his wagon home.

He sees the gray ash of a fire,
The water-filled rut of a wheel.
He finds the bee-heavy pit of a plum,
But his family and wagon are gone.

Far down the west-winding road,
The wagon lumbers on.
The children look back, through a tunnel of trees.
Will their golden Pawpaw come?

"He has run off," says the mother,
"To the wild free forest ways.
He will not follow us now,
As we follow the westering sun."

But in the wet green grass of the morning,
In the hot white gold of the sun,
Under the green and gold trees,
Pawpaw begins his run.

"Stop with me," says a girl,
As he streaks by her log-house door.
"I have milk for a gold cat to drink,
And a soft bed on the log-house floor."

But Pawpaw runs by the log-house girl.
Under the trees and out in the sun,
Over a brook and over a stone,
On and on he must run.

"Come with me, fast-running cat,"
Says a man with a coon cap and a gun.
"Far away, we will sleep under trees,
You will live free, if you come."

Pawpaw will not be free
With the coon-cap man and his gun.
Down the dark of the forest trail,
On and on, he must run.

A bear cub cries, "I'll catch you, cat,
Little gold cat who runs.
Then you will catch me; we'll play
Together all day in the sun."

But Pawpaw does not listen to the baby bear.
On and on he must run,
Over a log, over the grass,
In and out of the sun.

A red fox lopes by Pawpaw's side.
"Let's run together," he cries.
"I can run faster than any gold cat,
Come on, gold cat, and run."

They race where a woodchuck sits in the sun,
By his hole in the grassy mound.
The woodchuck whistles, the fox is gone.
And, alone, Pawpaw runs on.

The deer stand still to see him pass by,
They watch with wide, dark eyes.
His running frightens the tawny deer.
They jump and turn and are gone.

Down by the silent-wheeled wagon,
The children watch and wait.
"He will not come," sighs the mother.
"My darlings, he will not come."

Now the apricot sun glows low,
Birds are black in the flaming sky,
The log-cabin girl has locked her door,
The man in the coon cap rests his gun.

Old bear has found her wandering cub,
And the fox has lost his woodchuck gray.
As the darkness rolls up the hills,
The tired Pawpaw runs on and on.

The father waters the oxen,
And looks to the circling stars,
"We will move on in the morning.
Rest now, rest— and good-night."

CO. SCHOOLS
C698052

Then a tiger flash in the firelight!
From the darkness, a gold cat runs!
Straight to the children's arms he leaps!
"Mother! Mother! Our Pawpaw comes!"